Mel Bay Presents

Practice for Performance

for Cello and Related String Instruments

by

Daniel Morganstern

1 2 3 4 5 6 7 8 9 0

This book is dedicated to my dear friend and mentor, Henson Markham, with gratitude and affection.

Foreword

Practice for Performance hinges on one fundamental belief. When technique becomes an instinctive response to a musical imperative, more reliable and better performances result. I have often noticed that under the inspired leadership of a great conductor, orchestral musicians will transcend technical limitations and play beyond their normal capacities, and in the company of an inspired artist in chamber music situations, the playing of lesser musicians will often rise significantly.

In May of 1982, after being away for several years, Kenneth Schermerhorn walked into the pit of the Metropolitan Opera House to conduct a performance of *Swan Lake.* He faced a demoralized, desensitized, and disinterested orchestra that had not been sounding good for weeks. When, under his leadership, the principal oboist played the first poignant notes of the overture, the orchestra members knew that a dramatic change was taking place.

Maestro Schermerhorn delayed and elongated the second and fourth beats of the first several bars in order to give the oboist time to fill the huge hall with his sound. Maestro Schermerhorn supported the oboe solo with a heavier and more portentous accompaniment than we were accustomed to playing. By the time the overture ended we sounded like a first rate symphony orchestra.

Ray Still, now retired principal oboe of the Chicago Symphony Orchestra, was considered by many, including Jascha Heifetz with whom he recorded, to be one of the greatest oboists in the world. I was naturally very intimidated when, in 1967, he invited me to play music by Bach for voice, oboe, and cello. To my surprise, rather than feeling stiff and self-conscious, I was quickly immersed in the single musical impulse, which transformed the three people into one entity. The vision Mr. Still had of this magnificent music was so powerful and his sound and phrasing so absolute that only an equal response from the bass line seemed appropriate. To this day the experience remains undiminished, and epitomizes the premise of this book: When technique becomes a response to a musical imperative, execution improves both in fluency and control.

The examples in this book, both musical and non-musical, offer a foundation to help evoke instinctive musical responses in the mechanical processes of playing the cello, and have been advantageously applied by colleagues to other instruments as well.

Special thanks to my superb editors: Elaine Fine, William Ryden, and Dennis Friesen-Carper.

Daniel Morganstern

Contents

Leonard Rose

Introduction

I was extremely fortunate to meet the distinguished pianist Leonard Shure just as I was beginning my career as a professional musician. Mr. Shure's stepson, David, had been a student of mine for several months when Mr. Shure invited me to visit him at his Riverside Drive apartment in New York. Mr. Shure asked me about my aspirations. I told him that I wanted to get a technique that was so good and reliable that I would be able to play anything perfectly under any circumstances. He looked at me sadly and said "I hope you never get your great technique." "Why not?" I asked. "Because" he said, "you will be too easily satisfied with superficial excellence and leave many possibilities unexplored." "On the other hand," he continued, "if you work on a piece of music asking yourself constantly what does this music demand, note by note and phrase by phrase, and find a way to meet those demands, then your technique can be as infinite as the music." This inspiring conversation made a profound and lasting impression on me and created a powerful paradigm shift. I no longer viewed technique as a series of formulas by which I could conveniently and reliably get my fingers on the notes in front of me, but began to understand it as an organic process through which great thoughts and feelings could be translated into sound.

In no way did this approach cause me to undervalue perfect intonation, rhythm and beauty of sound; on the contrary, it greatly particularized each of these elements. Eventually I became keenly aware of the expressive possibilities created by bending notes *slightly* flatter or sharper to enhance emotional effects suggested by the underlying harmonic background of the music at hand, as well as the "ring of truth" that beautiful intonation gives to tonal quality. I put rhythm into a context of "tempo rubato," where subtle crescendos, diminuendos, accelerandos, and ritards breathe life into the music. I came to understand sound, the medium through which all musical messages flow, as a multi-faceted blend of volume, resonance, and timbre. I learned that a musical conception or idea encompasses all three elements; rhythm, pitch, and sound, each of which need to be brought into sharp focus. Bearing this in mind, the technical execution of a musical idea becomes an exact physical manifestation of that musical idea.

Mr. Shure offered to teach me in exchange for teaching David. I considered this a rather lopsided arrangement since Mr. Shure was one of the highest-priced piano teachers in New York and I was new to teaching. Because I was in total awe of his great musicianship and was not in a position to pay his regular fee, I accepted his offer.

During the next few years with Mr. Shure I learned some important facts about sonata playing. I learned that the Beethoven and Brahms sonatas are piano sonatas with an addition of a cello voice, *not* cello pieces with piano accompaniment. I also learned that no intelligent decision about how to play the cello part can be made without reference to the entire score; and every phrase has to make sense and come from details found in the score.

At my lessons we would work through some important piece very carefully. I would play a short segment and Mr. Shure would ask me why I chose to phrase it the way I did. He asked if it could be interpreted closer to what was in the score and would demonstrate what he had in mind at the piano. He played with a tonal opulence, emotional warmth and absolute rhythmic authority that exceeded my most utopian expectations. From this experience very different priorities emerged. The biggest change was in the value I placed on the middle and end of long notes and the opportunities they offered for emotional expression. In order to gain a clear understanding of how much of the subtle crescendos, diminuendos, accelerandos and ritards were required; I would practice each phrase in separated eighth and sixteenth notes (played with separate bows) at performance tempo and with full expression.

I found myself favoring fingerings that shifted on the same finger in cantabile passages creating a legato of the left hand rather than simply dropping a finger and using finger substitutions on repeated notes to enhance an emotional effect. In the bow I tried to create the effect of very long up and down bows, while changing the bow direction many times, by bringing every down bow closer to the frog in an up bow phrase and every up bow closer to the tip in a down bow phrase. At times Mr. Shure would play with me and those experiences sustain and inspire me to this day.

My first professional experiences were as principal cellist for both the American Ballet Theatre and the Lyric Opera of Chicago. I found myself responsible for many important cello solos, such as those in *Swan Lake, Sleeping Beauty, Giselle, Tosca, Don Carlo,* and *Masked Ball.* These and many other solos can be found in my excerpt book *Cello Solos from Opera and Ballet* published by International Music Company.

Due to a rigorous tour and performance schedule I was faced with the problem of trying to maintain a high standard of playing regardless of fatigue, poor acoustics, limited practice time and my tendencies to have good and bad days. I had the same problems later in my career touring with the American Chamber Trio. I learned that it was one thing to play well, and quite another to do it consistently. In order to be consistent, I had to assume that every day would be a bad day and I had to develop routines for sounding good, even on a bad day.

I developed a set of priorities for performing situations. I knew that I had to have accurate intonation, excellent rhythm, and a beautiful sound. Intonation is the one immutable element (no one can "interpret" his way out of bad pitch), but it is entirely possible, and often necessary, to bend rhythm in order to accommodate an accelerando or ritard. Still, the starting point must be metronomically accurate. The quality of the sound, its focus, resonance, volume, and timbre, comes after perfect intonation and excellent rhythm.

Since I played the same orchestral solos, piano trios, and solo pieces over and over again, I noticed that the caliber of a given performance always reflected the organization and practicing that preceded it. If I practiced a solo piece, an orchestral solo, or a chamber work in a context that resembled the ultimate performance conditions, it was always more effective for me at the "moment of truth" than it would have been if I had practiced the same work out of context.

In order to create a context, I used a small portable cassette recorder to record bass lines, vocal lines, violin lines, rhythmic subdivisions, or even words. I would play along with the resulting tape, and put myself in the position of teacher and student, soloist and accompanist, at the same time. This way of practicing turns the many mechanical processes involved in playing the cello (or any other instrument) into internal or organic responses.

The daily observation of, and collaboration with, great conductors and singers at the Chicago Lyric Opera profoundly shaped my thinking. Extraordinary conductors are able to elicit passionate and precise playing from an orchestra on a consistent basis because their movements are consistent. The musicians, reacting to the same stimulus each time, are able give the same musical response to that stimulus each time. I am also continually impressed by the magnificent singers who are able to project their beautiful and powerful voices to the uppermost balcony (the equivalent of a long city block).

During the years immediately preceding my Alice Tully Hall debut, I became extremely aware of my need to develop exact and premeditated conceptions of the music I played. I also needed to develop the ability to physically execute and project my conceptions in order to emulate the best qualities of the conductors and singers I admired.

This book contains various methodologies that evolved from my experiences. I make no claims that these techniques are the best and only ways to work, but they work for me and they work for many of my students. I hope they will be of value to others.

Daniel Morganstern

Part I
How I Studied the Cello

I had just turned sixteen when Leonard Rose accepted me as a student. At that point I had no idea of what the fine points of cello playing even were. I appeared for my first lesson with sonatas by Locatelli, Schubert, and Brahms. Mr. Rose reacted to my renditions with a not unkindly chuckle, and assured me that it would be years before I would be ready to do a credible performance of either the Locatelli or the Schubert. He thought the Brahms E minor sonata would do very nicely as a starting point, and went immediately to work, showing me how to hold the bow and sit at the cello.

I did not have a lesson the next Saturday because Mr. Rose was giving a recital at Washington Irving High School in Manhattan. This was one of the finest concert series in New York and was subsidized so that tickets were very affordable, even to high school students. Hearing that recital was the turning point of my cellistic life. Mr. Rose played a program of great classics which included the Beethoven D major sonata, the Bach C major Suite, and the Tchaikovsky "Rococo" Variations. He performed at a level of technical perfection, beauty of sound, and emotional warmth I had never even imagined possible. To me, playing like that seemed to be the only really worthwhile goal in life. In the intervening years Mr. Rose's standard of excellence and my desire to achieve it remained constant.

Mr. Rose's playing was as magnificent as I remember it. His recordings from that time, which include the Franck and Grieg sonatas, Schubert's "Arpeggione," the Boccherini A major and Sammartini sonatas, Ernest Bloch's *Schelomo,* the Saint-Saëns Concerto, the Brahms Double Concerto, the Beethoven Triple Concerto and Tchaikovsky's "Rococo" Variations with the New York Philharmonic, and radio broadcasts of the Alan Shulman's and Samuel Barber's Concertos (which are in my possession), indisputably confirm that fact.

I knew that I would always measure my own playing by that singularly worthwhile and utterly unattainable standard, giving me, at all times, a clear direction and uncompromising reality.

When I started studying with him, Leonard Rose was in the early stages of his solo career, having resigned five years earlier from the New York Philharmonic where he was principal cellist from 1944 to 1951. Mr. Rose was a very devoted teacher. He gave each of his Juilliard students 30 lessons a year, and he assigned more advanced students to work with his younger students, like me, when he was away on tour. As I reflect back, I can see the method he used to instill the value of perfect intonation, rhythm, and beauty of sound, the hallmarks of his own playing, in his students.

For my first fifteen lessons I worked on the first movement of the Brahms E minor Sonata. By demonstration and comments, Mr. Rose kept working on bridging the gap between his playing and mine. He was always kind and encouraging regardless of how wide that gap was, and within five or six months I believe that, based on my playing, it was possible for someone to identify me as one of his students.

The following summer I had the opportunity to study with Mr. Rose at the Meadowmount School of Music in upstate New York where Ivan Galamian taught violin, and Josef Gingold taught chamber music. At Meadowmount I worked on the Brahms Sonata and the Boccherini Concerto. The following fall I won the first prize in the Brooklyn Philharmonic youth competition playing the Boccherini, a piece that I learned in only eight lessons with Mr. Rose. While I was learning the Boccherini, I was also able, with Mr. Rose's help, to maintain the standards I had established for the Brahms. The greatness of Mr. Rose's teaching was his ability to establish a standard of excellence as the first constant. Once this constant was established, it became possible for his students to teach themselves.

Mr. Rose firmly believed and taught that every element of technique had to be mastered in exercises, etudes, and pieces of repertoire before it became internal and unconscious. He insisted on hearing three octave scales and etudes at every lesson, and I was expected to play everything by memory. Certain etudes took a long time for me to master, and Mr. Rose would not release me from them even if it took many months before I could play them to his satisfaction. By working this way I became aware of the value of persistence. As my Popper etudes improved I always found a corresponding improvement in my playing of music in the repertoire.

Playing for Mr. Rose always made me very nervous because, as I later realized, I was forced to hear myself through his ears. Painful as that experience was, it had two lifelong advantages. No performing experience, no matter how important, was as hard as playing for him. Eventually I got used to criticizing myself without losing either my temper or my self-confidence. It is impossible for me to overestimate the influence Mr. Rose exerted over my career. Every move I made was motivated by my intense desire to emulate his unequalled standard of excellence. His rigorous practice routines became models for my own, both in organization and length.

Mr. Rose's repertoire included the very best solo and chamber music works. By adopting his repertoire and avoiding lesser works, I was able to spend my time working on great music and bringing the solutions to the many technical and musical problems the works presented to the great cello solos in the opera and ballet repertoire. Mr. Rose defined possibilities that would have been impossible for me to imagine without his example.

After working with me for three years, Mr. Rose suggested that I study for a period of time with Luigi Silva, a cellist famous for his transcriptions of the Paganini 24 caprices and Kreutzer's 42 studies as well as editions of the Piatti and Servais Caprices. Mr. Rose, who worked on the Barber Concerto with Mr. Silva before playing it with Leonard Bernstein and the New York

Philharmonic, considered him a great authority on left-hand technique.

Mr. Silva had a wonderful way of organizing the left hand. I have incorporated many of his ideas in my scale system. Two of his basic concepts that have been useful to me include angling the left hand according to its function, and the organization of the left-hand position by the spaces between the fingers.

For cantabile playing Mr. Silva advocated angling the hand back for optimal vibrato. He called this the "violinistic" position. For chordal playing, he angled the hand forward towards the 4th finger, and called this position the "guitar" or hanging position. Mr. Silva had me hold the cello like a guitar and strum the chords of the Piatti Caprice No. 7 to give me a feel for this extremely useful technique. For general passage work, he advocated what he called the "square position" which, as its name implies, had the fingers fall at a 90° angle.

In his organization of the left hand by the spaces between the fingers, he divided the positions on the neck into three possible frames:

1. Closed position has half steps between all fingers.
2. Open position has a whole step between the first and second fingers, and half steps between the others.
3. Extended position has a step and a half between the first and second fingers and half steps between the others.

For thumb position the four most common frames are (- = whole step, u = half step):

1. whole, whole, half (- - u)
2. whole, half, whole (- u -)
3. half, whole, whole (u - -)
4. whole, whole, whole (- - -)

By memorizing the feel of each frame, eight notes (over two strings) will be securely in tune. This way of organizing the hand into frames is particularly valuable in both fast passage work and in playing double-stops.

While I studied with Mr. Silva, I spent many, many hours practicing double stops, scales, and etudes. He put a special emphasis on Gruetzmacher and Paganini. I believe that this work greatly improved the security and strength of my left hand.

When playing artificial harmonics Mr. Silva had me place my third finger between the A string and the D string resting the tip of the third finger on the fingerboard, so that the side of the finger touched the inside (D string side) of the A string. With my finger firmly down instead of resting lightly on the A string, my artificial harmonics were much more accurate. Discovering the space on the side of the string, and the secure wall the string provided, I found myself playing more and more on the inside of the string, gaining both security and accuracy.

While I was studying with him, Mr. Silva insisted that I study counterpoint. He had been a student of Otterino Respighi and Rosario Scalero (who taught Samuel Barber and Gian Carlo Menotti), and believed that every real musician should have this skill. He sent me to his friend Frederick Werle, (another student of Scalero), who became my drillmaster in the writing of canons. Although I never exhibited any talent for the art of composition, this training proved indispensable in my ability to hear several lines simultaneously.

Aside from my introduction to counterpoint, the long-term benefits of my studies with Mr. Silva were focused on his left hand organization. At every stage of my career I used fingerings articulated in the scale system found in the next chapter. The security these fingerings provide serves me well.

There were huge philosophical differences among the three teachers I have discussed. Leonard Shure believed that all technique should be derived from musical material. This approach, while critically important in executing convincing musical statements in sonatas is completely useless for me in Strauss and Wagner operas where the ultimate musical decisions are made by the conductor.

Luigi Silva's goal was to achieve a technique, removed from musical context that could be applied to any musical situation. I have found great use for his left hand organization when playing operas by Strauss, Wagner, and Berg. I also use it when playing chordal and double-stopped passages in solo repertoire.

Leonard Rose's goal was to develop technique that ensured beautiful tone, perfect intonation, and elegant phrasing under performance conditions. He was especially interested in the execution of melodic passages and worked incessantly on tone production, bow distribution and emotional commitment. He had a high regard for the continuous maintenance of both his technique and his repertoire, and practiced many hours every day even on pieces he had played most of his life.

Although I organized most of my left hand technique based on Silva's ideas, Mr. Rose's influence helped me most in performing situations: being at my best today on today's solo was critical for me. Mr. Rose assumed that he would not be at his best unless he practiced constantly. I found this to be absolutely true for me too.

Further Study

Some years after my graduation from Juilliard I made a decision that upgraded my playing significantly. I had already performed most of the major operas of Wagner, Verdi, Strauss and Berg, and the ballets of Stravinsky, Prokofiev and Tchaikovsky. I had also given two solo recitals at Alice Tully Hall in New York. All my experience convinced me that when it came to sound, articulation and physical comfort, every gain I could make improved my chances for success and longevity as a cellist.

I called Mr. Rose and asked him to advise me on how to improve several aspects of my playing. By this time Mr. Rose's career was in full swing and he was constantly pressed for time. As usual, however, his natural generosity prevailed, and he did find time to work with me as circumstances allowed.

In order to maximize this work he suggested that I play on a regular basis for his longtime associate Channing Robbins, who had taught at the Juilliard School for many years.

Mr. Robbins was a great teacher. He studied with Leonard Rose and Felix Salmond (who also taught Leonard Rose, Frank Miller, Bernard Greenhouse, and Samuel Mayes), as well as Emmanuel Feuermann, and D.C. Dounis, and had innumerable solutions to every conceivable problem. He always answered my questions about technique to my satisfaction and my ultimate benefit. His advice about every aspect of cello playing was invaluable.

The approach of each of my teachers had unique advantages in certain situations, though none covered all the bases absolutely.

Luigi Silva

Part II: Scales

Like many people I find scales a very efficient and effective way to keep my playing agile and accurate. The following scale system covers many ways of practicing scales against a bass line. I use the three-octave scale itself as a bass line to put me in a context where volume, pitch, and rhythm are an instinctive response to a musical imperative.

The patterns I play incorporate long sustained notes, bow changes, rhythmic patterns, and incrementally faster scales (with more and more notes on a single bow), making shifts, and holding positions. By using a recorded bass line and playing along with the resulting tape, I put myself in a context of time (given by the metronome), pitch (given by the bass line), and sound (given by the volume at which I set my tape machine). Because I know exactly how long the tape lasts I can allocate my time intelligently.

Before showing how to play the scales against the pre-recorded bass line, I offer some preparatory examples to demonstrate Silva's way of setting positions and shifting from one position to another. These are illustrated in examples found in Sections II and III. In the interest of clarity, Silva's positions (open, closed, and extended) refer only to the hand frame which acts horizontally across the strings.

Section I. The bass line

This is the E major scale in whole notes. This is what I record onto a cassette. I use two preparatory notes so that I am well set to play with a full sound when I play my variations against it.

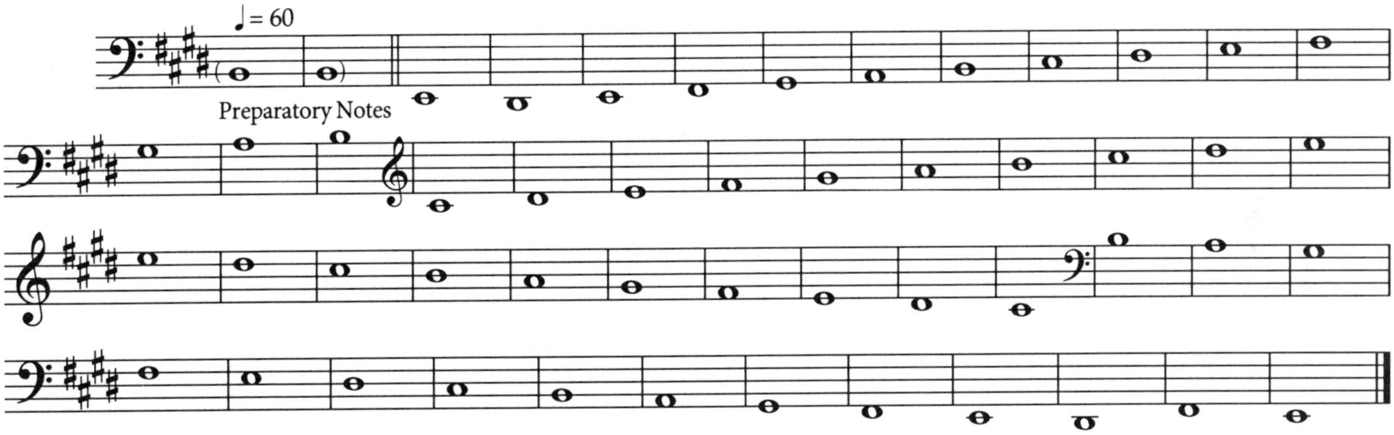

Section II. Trilling double stops, shifting, and fast moving scales

Example **II-A** takes the position of E F♯ G♯ (an open position) and places the first, second, and fourth fingers on the G string, and the third finger on the C string. The first and third fingers are held down, while the second and fourth fingers are trilled. These trilling exercises set the feel of the position.

In Example **II-B** the first three notes of the scale are played as fast as possible ascending and descending many times. If the position has been well set, the intonation will be stable because the fingers will be lifting and dropping in a well-set frame.

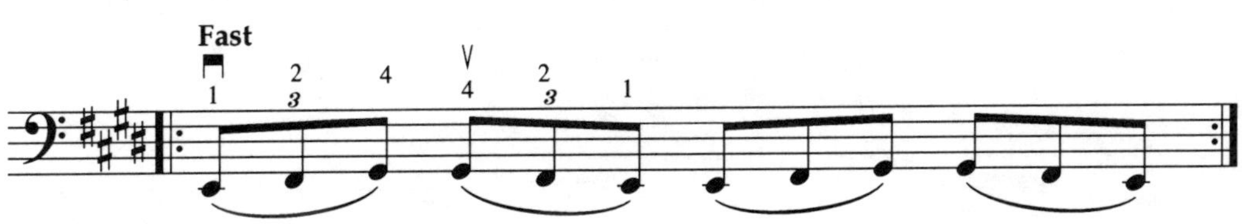

Example **II-C** is in the next position and uses the trilling patterns described in II-A.

In **Example II-D,** the hand moves from the E F♯ G♯ position to the A B C♯ position smoothly by shifting back on the C string (the fourth finger on G♯ moves to F♯).

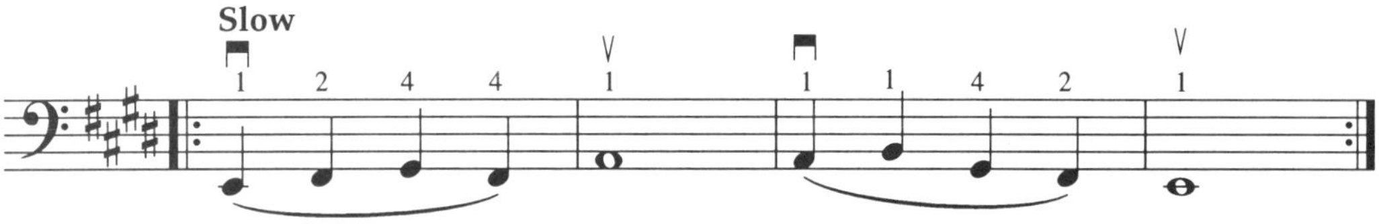

Example **II-E** moves rapidly through the first six notes of the scale ascending and descending: As in Example II-B, if the positions are well set, the intonation will remain stable. It is important to realize that in fast playing there is virtually no time to adjust pitch, so having the position set in advance guarantees much better accuracy.

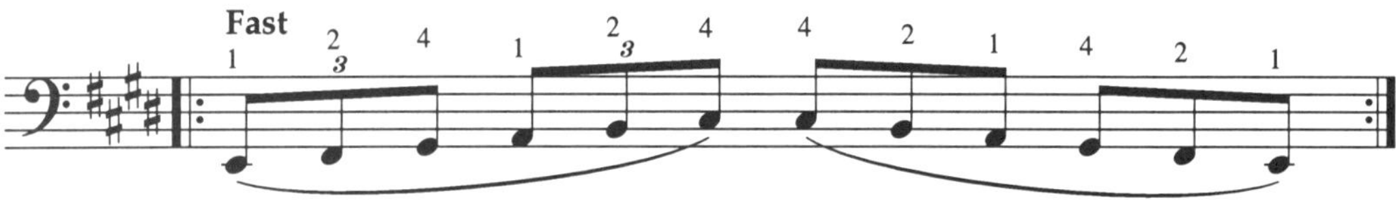

Example **II-F** bridges the A B C♯ position (on the G string) with the following D♯ E F♯ position.

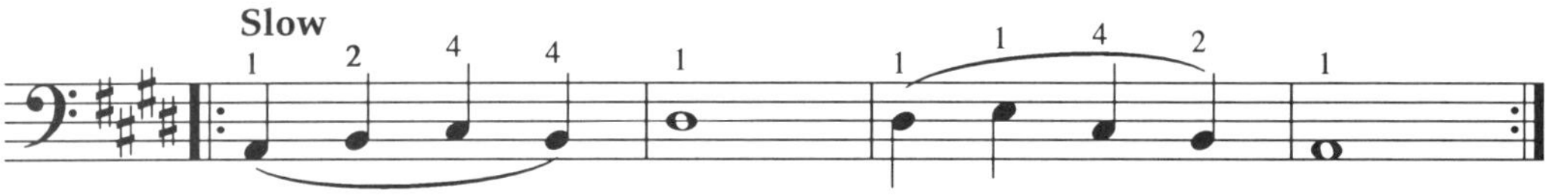

The rest of the examples follow the established pattern. The underlying principle is that every shift should move from position to position rather than from finger to finger.

Section III. The E major scale with added helper notes

Section III takes the entire E major scale in half notes with added helper notes. As written, it will work well against a bass line scale with eight whole note E's added to the end. Playing this example in half notes (Example **III-A**) will allow two passes through the scale against the tape. Played in quarter notes (Example **III-B**), it will allow four passes. If it is played in eighth notes (Example **III-C**), it can be played eight times against the tape. I have found this exercise particularly valuable in setting both the intonation and the physical comfort of the hand.

III-A

III-B

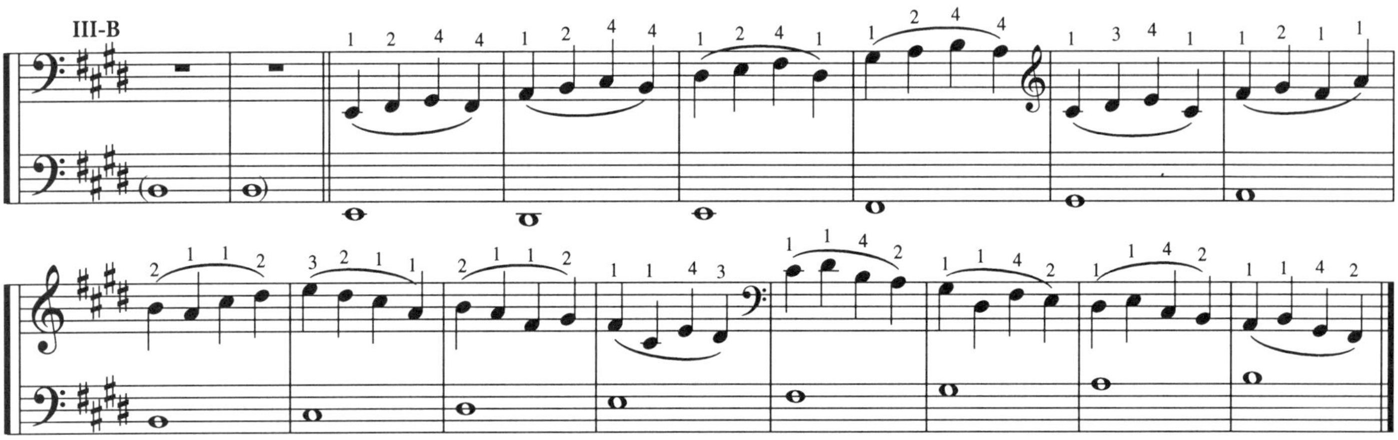

III-C

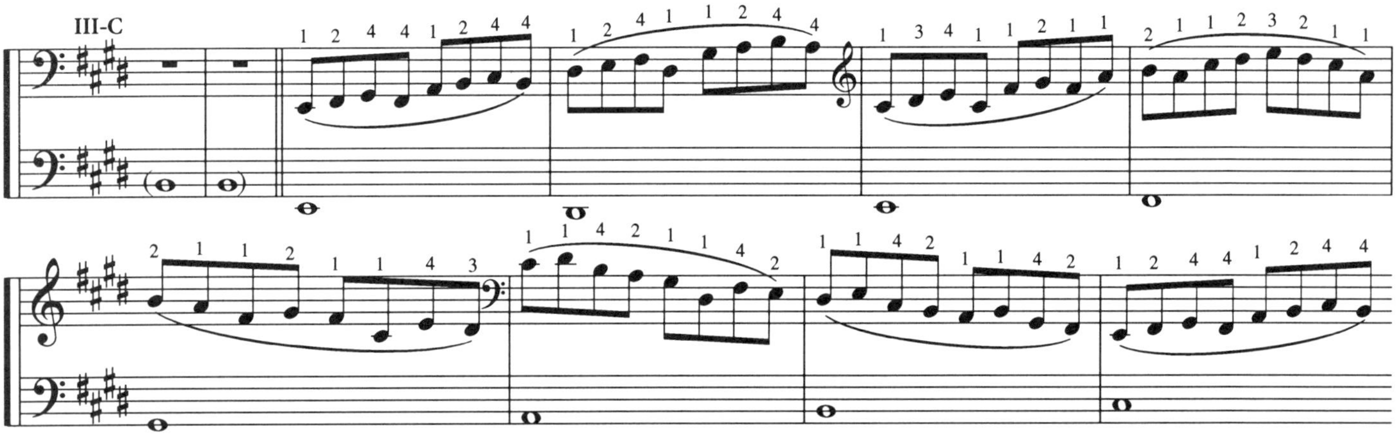

Section IV. Two diverse rhythmic patterns

When I was studying the Tchaikovsky "Rococo" Variations with Leonard Rose and Channing Robbins, Mr. Robbins suggested that I play the entire third variation, a slow cantabile melody, at the volume of the loudest note. This made an interesting connection to a comment made by Michelangelo, who said that the statue he was sculpting was *in* the marble, and his job was to cut away everything that wasn't *Moses* or *David.* By practicing at the volume of the loudest note, subtle nuances can be created by subtracting rather than by adding sound. This allows us to gain flexibility instead of becoming tense and unmusical. Mr. Robbins worked hard with me to get a feel for what he called "forte pressure."

Leonard Rose used the two diverse rhythmic patterns given in Section IV as excellent ways to keep even bow pressure through notes of differing values. The object here is to keep the bow pressure and bow speed constant, regardless of how many notes are under a bow, while also keeping the speed and pressure constant through the shifts and string changes. Playing these patterns against the bass line scale provides a context where volume, pitch, and rhythm become an instinctive response to a musical imperative. It in effect creates a musical block of marble from which a statue can be cut.

IV-1A

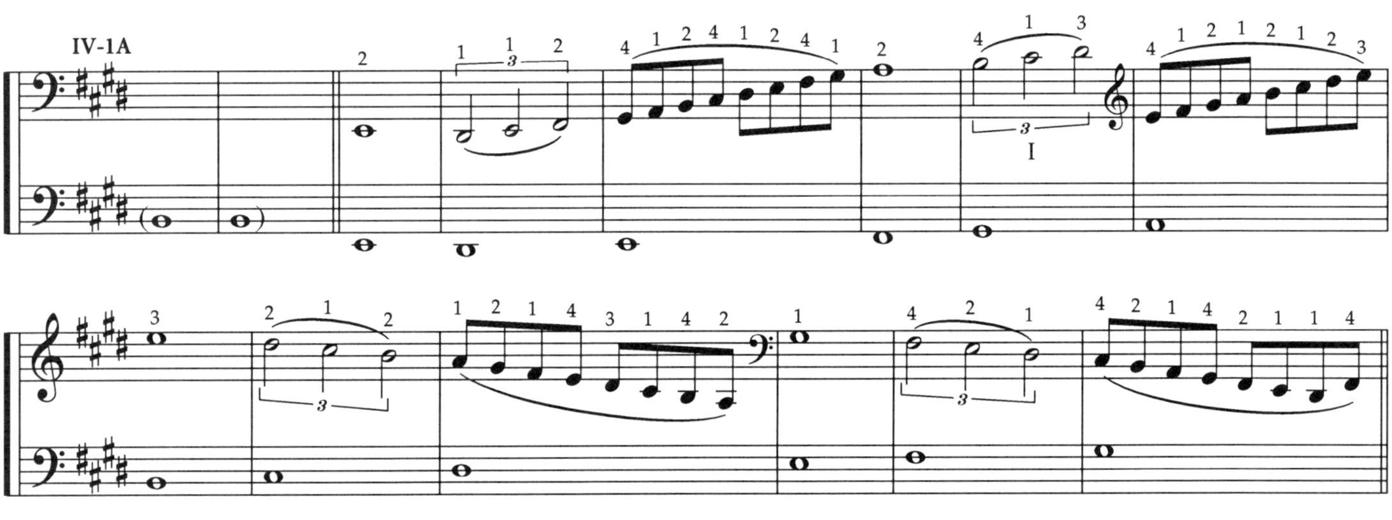

IV-1A cont.
IV-1B
etc.
IV-1C
etc.
IV-1D
etc.

IV-1E

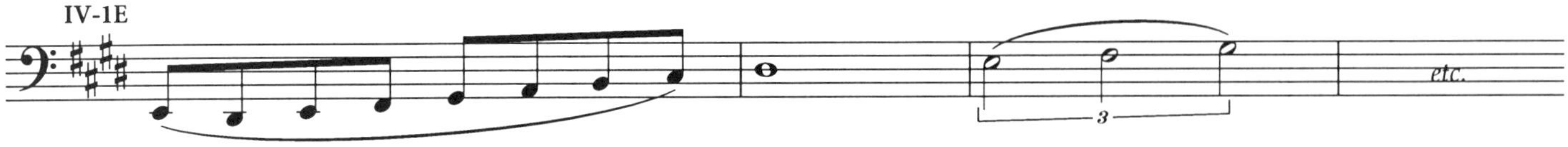

IV-1F

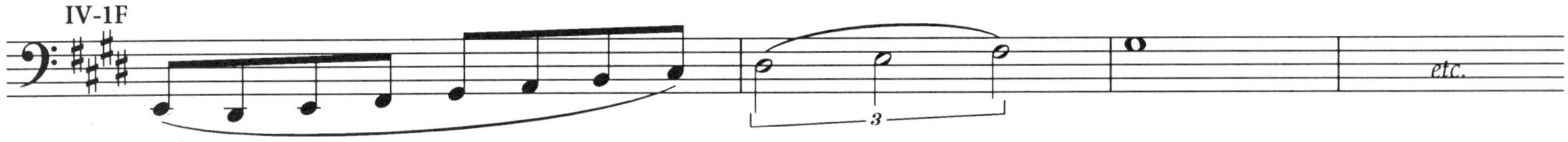

IV-2A

IV-2B

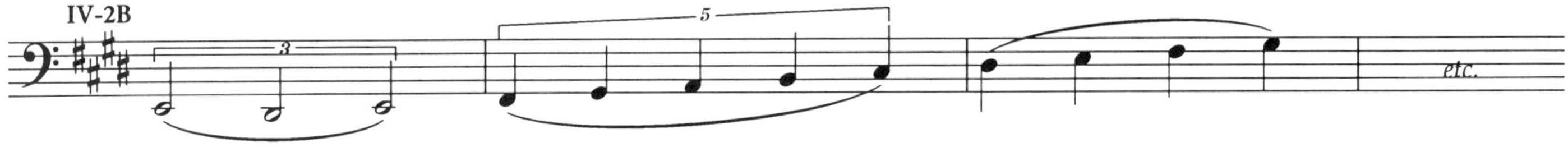

IV-2C

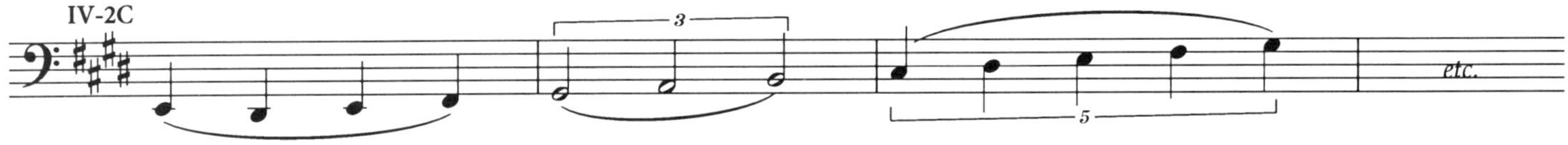

IV-2D

IV-2E

IV-2F

Section V. Scale of D.C. Dounis to develop forte pressure and endurance

The four octave C major scale shown in Section V was given to Mr. Robbins by D.C. Dounis. At 60 to the half note, it takes seven and a half minutes before the pattern returns to the original 3 notes. At first Mr. Robbins had me play the scale *mezzo-piano,* and then he had me play it *mezzo-forte.* Eventually I was able to play *forte* for seven and a half minutes without getting tense. When I transposed the scale up a half a step to D flat major, Mr. Robbins commented that I was "coming up in the world."

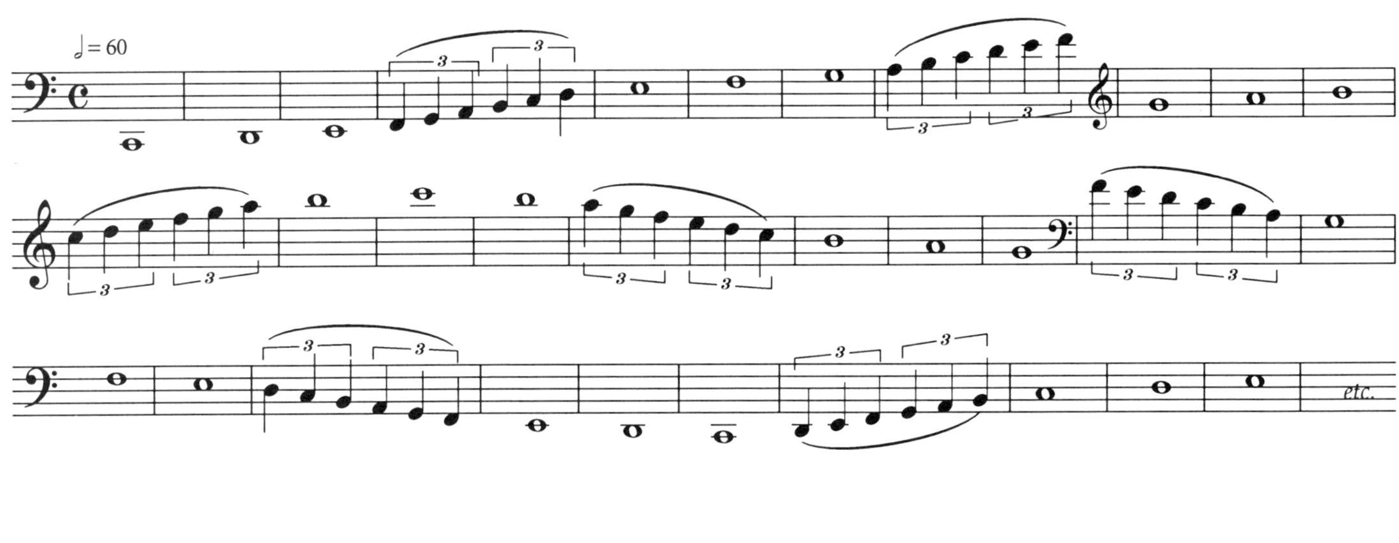

Section VI. Incrementally faster scale patterns

In Section VI, I use incrementally faster scales to train my hand to balance on the playing finger for optimal vibrato in the half notes, half note triplets, and quarter notes. By the time I am playing six, eight, or twelve notes on a single bow, holding positions becomes the major focus.

VI-A ♩= 60

VI-B

VI-C

VI-D

VI-E

VI-F

Section VII. Long tones and bow changes

Section **VII-A** is an excellent way to work on sustaining sound and playing with vibrato.

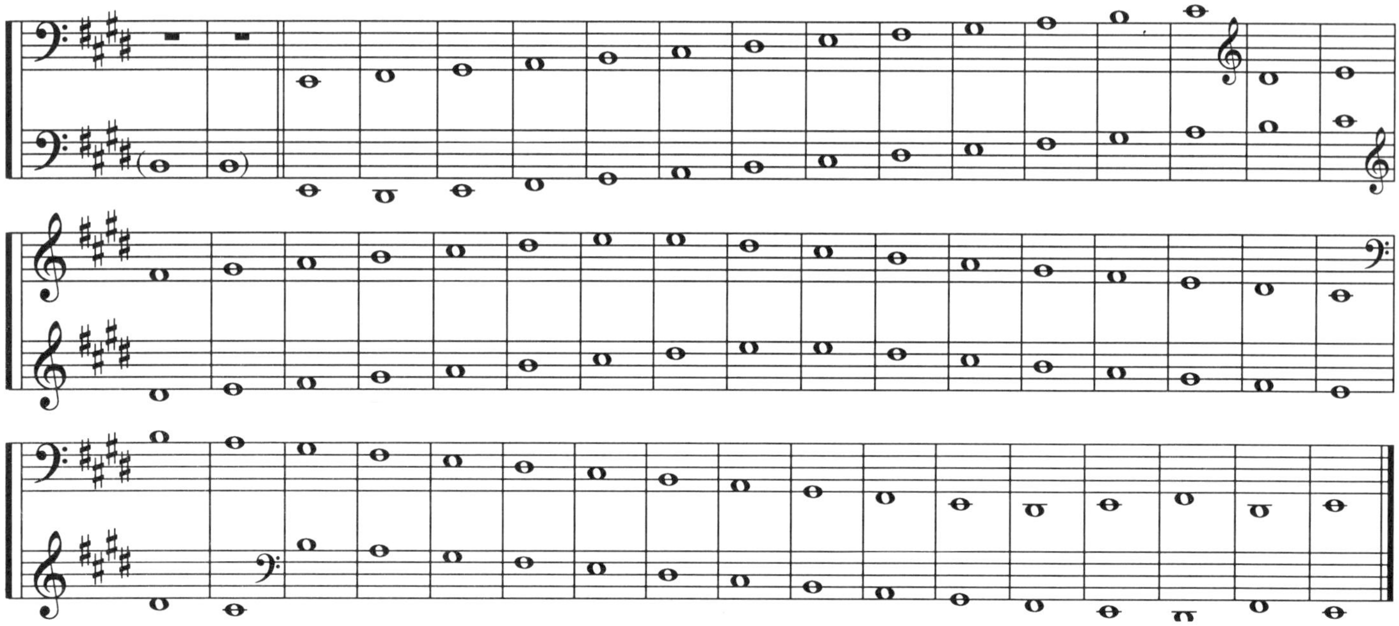

Section **VII-B,** with its suspensions over the bar line, counteracts the tendency to stop the bow before a bow change by creating a musical imperative that suggests swelling into the bow change.

The (1,3,8) scale and the incrementally faster scales can be practiced with separate bows advantageously. It is also valuable to practice these scales with reverse bowings.

In order to achieve perfect balance on a given finger Mr. Robbins had me play pizzicato maintaining the vibrato and ring of the note as long as possible. In performing this action the finger would find its position of balance because any other position other than the optimally balanced position would be uncomfortable. This action makes the other fingers line up in support of the vibrating finger. I find practicing slow scales pizzicato is a wonderful preparatory exercise for slow scales with the bow.

Part III
Creating a Context

In Part II I have attempted to show how putting scales in a musical context helped me to maintain and improve the vital elements of my playing, intonation, sound, and rhythm, as well as the technical means by which these elements are physically created.

In the Left Hand

1. Balance of fingers on long notes.
2. Holding of positions in faster moving notes.
3. Shifting from position to position rather than finger to finger.

In the Right Hand

1. Equalizing speed, pressure and spot on the string.

Since I knew that playing through the scale six times at the rate of half note = 60 took twelve and a half minutes, it was always possible to allocate my scale time intelligently and have a good idea of where I would end up technically (even on a bad day). When I went on tour with the ballet, the trio, or when touring with a recital program, I often implemented this contextual method by using headphones. I would put one headphone over my right ear and leave the other ear without one so that I could hear both the bass line and myself. In this chapter I will discuss effective solutions to different performing situations I came up against using a contextual method.

Play from beginning to end

Early in my career I was engaged by the Northern Virginia Music Center at Reston, Virginia as "Artist in Residence." In addition to coaching the cello section in the orchestra and various student string quartets, I was a member of the Reston Trio, which performed weekly recitals during each of the six weeks we were in session, and I played a concerto with the orchestra each summer. The orchestra was fairly good and we often had excellent soloists such as Aaron Rosand, the great violin virtuoso and Morley Merideth, a famous bass-baritone from the Metropolitan Opera. Our concerts were sometimes reviewed in the Washington D.C. papers like the *Washington Post* and the *Washington Evening Star,* and commentaries were made over WGMS, the area's fine arts radio station.

For me this exposure was a double-edged sword. If I got a good review from one of these papers, I could upgrade my credibility. This was important for me because I had not yet made my New York debut.

As luck would have it, my first ever performance of the Schubert "Arpeggione" sonata and first ever performance of the Haydn D major Concerto came in the same week. I don't think I need justify my apprehension to any cellist. As the concert dates came closer, I found myself unprepared. The ensuing panic gave me an insight that not only saved the concerts for me but also served as a method for dealing with all performing situations. I realized that I had habitually practiced practicing and now needed to practice playing. That meant beginning to end without stopping just like a performance. Fortunately I was still in New York and unencumbered with other work when the light went on in my brain.

I called Gordon Steel, a fine pianist and good friend, and asked him to play through these works with me. I put a microphone in the piano with the lid down and recorded straight through both pieces. For the next week I played through each piece three times a day with the tape before working on any details. By the third time there weren't many details to work on. I found that many problems solved themselves and many difficulties were simply eliminated by the forward motion. Also, I found myself anticipating problems much longer in advance.

The experience of playing through with the piano tape was so similar to the "first" performances that during those performances I felt as if I were playing my twentieth performances instead of my first. I was, in fact, well reviewed in the *Star* and had a usable quote for my Tully Hall debut flyer.

I have used and taught this method of practicing ever since. It has greatly increased my ability to handle large amounts of repertoire and to find practical solutions to difficulties. Being in the middle of a performance (simulated or otherwise) is the best way to find out what works and when necessary to make a musical virtue out of a technical vice.

In contrast to this way of practicing, I have found that working endlessly on small segments tends to distort our view of their importance. Playing from beginning to end without stopping, in a context similar to the anticipated performance, homogenizes the piece so that no one passage seems that much more difficult than any other. I have found no better way to prepare orchestral solos. The sudden and short-lived transition that a principal player must make from being an orchestra player to being a soloist is often unnerving. By playing a given solo over many times in a context that demands full expression (such as a bass line) this problem is mitigated to a large degree because the solo becomes the most familiar music of the evening. Mr. Rose spoke of playing entire recitals for imaginary audiences as part of his conditioning, and it is the *conditioning aspect* of playing from beginning to end without stopping that is so valuable.

Conception and execution

In a *Newsweek* article about Vladimir Horowitz, the pianist Alfred Brendel defined playing of genius. He said "playing of genius is when the music is at the same time correct and bold. The correctness says 'this is the way it must be.' But the boldness surprises and overwhelms us with the way it can be - what we thought was impossible becomes true."

The element of rhythm is the very meeting place of the correct and the bold. Correctness is perceived by balance and inevitability of a phrase, and boldness is defined by the degree of accelerando, ritard, crescendo, or diminuendo we are able to bring to bear on a phrase without distorting the balance or inevitability.

It is easy to get a sense of this from the discipline of acting. When I was in high school, I heard many unconvincing versions of Hamlet's soliloquy that begins "To be or not to be." Sir Laurence Olivier, on the other hand, rendered the passage with so much conviction and authority that the words receded into the background while the issues of mortality and the human condition dominated my perception.

It is possible to live in a musical environment of genius by listening to recordings of great artists on a regular basis. Four of my favorite artists are Jascha Heifetz, Artur Rubinstein, Luciano Pavarotti, and Leonard Rose. There are, of course, many great artists to hear on recordings, and all of them demonstrate correctness and boldness together. I also find that a steady listening diet of rubato playing and singing widens my parameters of acceptable interpretive expansion. Channing Robbins often referred to a particular school of thought that stressed playing as loud as possible, as soft as possible, as fast as possible, or as slow as possible. I tried this technique while playing the Tchaikovsky "Rococo" Variations, and to my surprise, it proved effective if not in the best taste. I mention this experience to urge those bound by restrictive conceptions of good taste to open their minds and free their imaginations.

Leonard Shure always stressed phrase direction as the first order of interpretive business. The two possible directions were leading or falling. In a leading phrase a group of notes move forward in an accelerando (possibly very slight), and in a falling phrase a group of notes comes from a point in a ritard, losing energy until it comes to rest. Often a long phrase is kept alive by moving forward and falling backward several times. The main thing is to avoid static metronomic accuracy devoid of direction.

Many times I have heard artists move a phrase forward, accelerating ahead of the metronomic beat, and then taking all the accumulated time to play a single long note and hold it for a satisfyingly long time. At the point that the metronomic beat catches up, the phrase continues with inevitability and grace.

In the year that preceded my Alice Tully Hall debut, and for the next couple of years, I had the opportunity to work with the violinist Gerald Beal. He taught me a way to practice that focused my attention absolutely on the movements of a phrase and the exploitation of all its long notes. Gerald Beal would conduct me through everything that I played for him while he sang and clapped out subdivisions that helped me to focus my attention on the direction and structure of the phrase I was playing. (See Musical Examples 1, 2, and 3). In the second theme of the first movement of the Dvorak Concerto (Musical Example 1), the subdivided eighth notes support the full length of the half note, and then release, allowing the following eighth notes to move freely. In the fifth bar, I subdivide the first two quarter notes of the dotted half note with eighth notes, and I subdivide the second part of the dotted half and the quarter note that follows with triplet eighth notes. This kind of subdivision helps me to achieve increasing intensity during long notes.

In the first theme of the Schubert "Arpeggione" Sonata (Musical Example 2), I chose to syncopate my subdivisions in order to energize the half note motion, which has a tendency to be static.

In the opening statement of *Ein Heldenleben* (Musical Example 3), I subdivide the first half note into triplets. The sixteenth note subdivisions of the third beat in the second, third, and fourth measures anticipate the rhythm and tempo of the faster moving notes that come on the fourth beat of each measure. This kind of subdivision helps achieve an absolutely even transition from the slow-moving notes to the fast-moving notes. Paying attention to inner subdivisions changed my relationship to the instrument distinctly. Rather than concentrating on actions concerned with manipulating the instrument while playing, my attention turned to reacting to clapped rhythmic subdivisions. This made thinking the active ingredient in my playing, and caused what came out of the cello to be a reaction or consequence of my thinking. Additionally, after I adopted this way of practicing, a crystal clear image (like an architectural blueprint) of the music emerged, and I was able to learn and memorize much greater amounts of repertoire than I ever could before.

By playing my pieces from beginning to end with tapes that had my teacher clapping subdivisions while I played, I was able to prepare and play three New York recitals in one year. My programs included both Brahms Sonatas and the Clarinet Trio, the second and fifth Bach Suites, the Beethoven A major Sonata, the Schubert "Arpeggione" Sonata, the Tchaikovsky "Rococo" Variations, the Fauré *Elegy,* and sonatas by Francoeur and Boccherini. I got three excellent reviews from "tough" critics that focused mainly on my musical presentation. *This would have seemed inconceivable to me one year earlier.*

I was certainly sold on this methodology but I needed a way to implement it without having to rely on another person, so I decided to sing and clap phrases myself into a cassette recorder and play along with the resulting tape. After playing with a tape a number of times I could sound convincingly the way I wanted to without the tape. Using this method of practice it is possible to work separately on conception and on execution, and to internalize the result.

I consider the use of subdivision to be an immensely powerful tool that enables a musician to absolutely control the destiny of a phrase and focus attention through the entire length of every note. It is the most compelling musical imperative and evokes the most powerful instinctive responses. *Turning the act of playing from action to reaction improves execution radically. Also, phrases can be structured to favor strength and conceal weakness.* The principles of using irregular subdivisions are to add more subdivisions when making a ritard, to eliminate them in an *a tempo* or an accelerando, and to subdivide a long note into units of the faster-moving notes that follow it in order to make smooth transitions.

Using syllables

I once played the opening solo cadenza in Verdi's *Ballo en Maschera* with Christoph von Dohnanyi conducting. Dohnanyi insisted that I play the solo in an uncongenial manner, and conducted it to make sure I did it his way. As a result of the tension I felt, my bow began to shake. The resulting "Hora Staccato" version of the solo was so mortifying to me that I needed to solve this problem immediately.

My solution was to syllabalize the notes of the solo with words that would focus my attention on the requirements of that solo. (See Musical Example 4.) My first objective for the *Ballo* solo was to keep my bow in the string, and my second objective was to vibrate all the notes. For the rest of the rehearsals and for all the performances I silently said the words "Keep the bow in the string, keep the bow in the string, always vibrate, always vibrate, always vibrate every note." When I did this my execution was excellent and the responsibility of interpretation fell on Maestro Dohnanyi. I have used this technique many times and it has always worked because, for some reason, my body does what the words tell it to do. As in my experience with the *Ballo* solo, most of the difference between sounding like an artist and sounding like a student is defined by the characteristics of sustained sound (without skimming) and a constant vibrato, particularly on the full length of long notes.

Channing Robbins often said that as soon as we experience discomfort, something in the brain switches off the ear, and we are unable to hear our musical malefactions. It seems that paying attention to what the music requires at the moment it is happening is a difficult skill to master. For me, the use of words eliminates that problem because as soon as I hear the notes (always before I play them) the words pop into my mind and my body obeys the commands. It has never been a problem for me to switch the verbiage on or off.

When I returned to study with Leonard Rose and Channing Robbins in my thirties I had a lot of revising to do. With my teachers' permission, I would record all my lessons. After I listened to the tape several times, I would syllabalize the pieces and etudes with reminders to keep the shoulder down, go out with the bow on down bows and in on up bows, feel the fingers on the bow, and watch the intonation. I made a rapid transition from having bad habits to having good ones.

When I teach I insist on recording all lessons so that my students can judge for themselves whether or not there is justice in my remarks. When they are listening they are also unencumbered by the need to impress me, and are able to hear their own playing and my remarks (usually for the first time). Many of my students have benefited from the verbal method to focus their attention on the music at hand.

Rhythm and tempo

Although I have stated that metronomic accuracy will not create elegant phrases, nothing of merit can take place unless we start with it. It has been said, "the good is the enemy of the best." This is true only if we do not move beyond it.

I believe implicitly in practicing passages while "notching" up the metronome incrementally from slower to faster tempos. Doing this saved my career. Shortly after I graduated from Juilliard I became principal cellist for the American National Opera Company, an organization created by Sarah Caldwell. The orchestra included flutist John Wummer, horn player Rudolph Puletz Jr. (both were formerly principal players in the New York Philharmonic), oboist Ray Still, the principal oboist of the Chicago Symphony, and many other young players who went on to hold principal positions in major American orchestras.

Our repertoire consisted of three operas: Puccini's *Tosca,* Verdi's *Falstaff,* and Berg's *Lulu.* Our production of *Lulu* was one of the first staged performances of the opera in the United States and many noted musicians (including Leonard Bernstein) attended the performances. We held our rehearsals and first performances in Indianapolis, Indiana. When I saw the impossibly complicated music of Berg's *Lulu* at the first rehearsal, I panicked.

I was totally at sea and felt the sharp little bites of fear attacking my insides. My assistant, Yuan Tung, encouraged me with comments like "you don't look too good," and "I'm worried about you." When I returned to my "flea bag" hotel room, I knew that I would either master the many difficult Lulu solos or resign ignominiously. It occurred to me that at an extremely slow tempo I could read anything. I figured out how slow I needed to start and notched every section up to tempo. By the time every section was up to tempo my rhythm, pitch, and sound were absolute. I had also memorized large sections. I followed this procedure for the next week, keeping myself slightly ahead of the progress of the orchestra. Many players in the orchestra complimented me, saying that I sounded like my teacher, Leonard Rose, and Yuan Tung stopped worrying about me.

I always return to "notching" when I play Strauss, Wagner, and Berg, as well as all my solo music, so that I can be absolutely solid in situations where my income and/or my reputation are at stake.

For my first recital tour with Eric Larsen we programmed the Rachmaninoff Sonata. Eric was being considered for a major faculty position at the North Carolina School for the Arts, which was one of our recital venues. Of course Eric and I both knew that our performance there would either count for or against his getting the job. Eric, who had inadequate time to practice, found the fourth movement impossible to play reliably. Remembering my orchestral experiences, I suggested that we take the worst section and notch it starting at 40 beats per minute. Ninety minutes later Eric could play the most difficult part of the movement solidly. He did make a good impression in our performance, and got the job.

Now, thanks to my influence, all his students are required to do "metronome duty" and several have won important international competitions.

Working this way, Eric and I benefited greatly from hearing all the notes of a piece at a slow tempo. Notching became more of a process of hearing than of playing. I would even record "notching" with Eric so that I could practice with the tapes when he wasn't with me.

Sound and bow arm development (using bass lines)

One of Channing Robbins maxims was "over tone, under tempo," which means that a reserve of tone can be created by practicing slower and louder than the dynamics and tempo of a piece demand. Subtracting sound to create nuances results in greater flexibility while pushing for more sound stiffens the body. In order to achieve a bigger sound without pushing, I practice with a slow piano tape with the volume on the tape recorder turned up. When I was working on developing my bow arm with Leonard Rose and Channing Robbins I concentrated on movements from the fifth Bach Cello Suite. I would compose a bass line, record it, and play with the resulting tape. (See Musical Examples 5, 6, and 7) Thereby I had a combination of inspired music in a context that demanded volume, bite, and energy. Practicing this way also improved my detache bow stroke. I made a notched bass line tape for the exposition of Paganini's *Moto Perpetuo* that I use for practicing various bowings. Of course I know exactly how long these tapes last, so I can allocate my practice time intelligently.

Melody and accompaniment

I once had a student who was unable to play a phrase in Bloch's Schelomo freely. My bass line accompaniments would usually work to free up a musical student's playing, but in this case it didn't work. Finally, in desperation, I asked her to play the bass line while I played the melody. We reversed parts several times, and eventually she was able to play the phrase freely. From this experience I discovered that the feel for a phrase is contained in all its parts, both the melody and its accompaniment, since they move together.

Orchestral applications

Early in my career, before I realized that an opera was more than just a cello part, I used to practice my parts by notching the hard parts and reading the rest. I had cause to worry about the (good or bad) impression I made because at the Lyric Opera we had a great deal of rehearsal time and demanding and often sarcastic conductors.

My application of the contextual method of playing in solo and chamber music changed my way of preparing orchestral material radically. When I began to use recordings to provide a context for my preparation, I found that it gave me several advantages over my old method of preparation.

When I had a context I knew exactly where my best attention would be required, and could use a red pencil to mark it in my part, I knew the approximate tempo. I also knew how the cello part related to the score, and could establish fingerings and bowings that would fill the requirements of the moment.

Part IV
Non-Contextual Practicing

It is enormously useful and effective to practice in a context that focuses attention on the problem at hand (playing from beginning to end, subdividing, using words, bass lines, and piano accompaniments), but it does not solve every problem. In the next section I will discuss the development and maintenance of mechanical skills (commonly called "technique") that are necessary for playing in tune, and playing with rhythmic control. I will also discuss tone production and offer some strategies for dealing with particular problems.

In 1975 Joan Sutherland sang the title role of *Lucia* at the Lyric Opera. Her execution of even the most difficult passages was so astonishingly accurate and emotionally overpowering at every performance that I felt compelled to ask her how she did it. In response to my questions she assured me that the big secret was that there were no secrets, and that she endeavored to sing perfectly in time and perfectly in tune so that any liberty she might take would be made from strength and not from weakness. Since none of this was news to me I was starting to feel somewhat disappointed when she said something really valuable. "In any passage or cadenza, there are only a few notes that are excruciatingly difficult - those are the ones I work on all the time."

Hearing this statement made me realize that there are many grades of difficulty and each one requires a different approach. For me it is analogous to housecleaning. Some things require only dusting, others mopping, but the really bad stuff needs scouring with steel wool and Ajax.

In this chapter I would like to present several ways of practicing small segments that are particularly difficult. This is very important because we want our execution to be even and homogenous. If one passage is more difficult than another it is better if the audience doesn't know it.

Practice forward and backward

For me, the single best technique for working out anything difficult is to play forward and backward. I usually play the first two notes back and forth several times then add the third note, the fourth, and so on, until I have all the notes in the passage. The notes and bowings reverse on the backwards segment but I keep the rhythm the same in both directions. This is particularly valuable in solos with big shifts such as the ones that occur in *Ariadne auf Naxos* and *La Sylphide* (see Musical Examples 8 and 9). In these solos the problem is exacerbated by the fact that one has to wait until they occur in the course of an opera or ballet. When it finally does occur there is a sudden and short-lived transition from orchestral player to soloist. At that moment of exposure, the shift (difficult to begin with) must be executed "cold" in front of one's colleagues, employer, and a large audience.

Before employing this back and forth practicing I would be more involved in my apprehension over the outcome than anything else. By using this technique to warm up the shift in question, the process of shifting, sustaining sound, and vibrating became mechanical and predictable and not emotional. Because of this I found myself more confident at the "moment of truth." For whatever reason, the back and forth process seems to homogenize a group of notes so that the most difficult maneuver feels as secure as the easiest. This method can be applied to etudes and passages efficaciously (see Musical Example 10, Popper Etude no. 26).

Channing Robbins was a distinguished professor of cello at the Juilliard School where he assisted Leonard Rose in teaching such world-class talents as Yo Yo Ma and Lynn Harrell as well as many other highly gifted cellists. For that reason I feel comfortable passing on some of his advice.

Mr. Robbins believed that any method of practicing that would make a passage *more difficult*—resulted in greater security when returning to the original version. Any of his former students will recognize the following list.

1. Practice everything with reverse bowings
2. Practice in each third of the bow
3. Practice one octave higher
4. Practice one octave higher with reverse bowings.

Those students who followed this advice usually found themselves with unprecedented security.

The reversed bowings have the effect of evening out the feel of the bow from frog to tip. Also, many times the reverse bowing was better than the original choice.

Practicing in each third of the bow has the effect of intensifying the sound and develops greater comfort in every part of the bow, especially in the upper half. It also produces a great sense of freedom when the whole bow is used.

Practicing one octave higher has the benefit of bringing the bow closer to the bridge. Upon returning to the original octave it is much easier to keep the bow closer to the bridge which has the advantage of producing a more intense and penetrating sound. I find this particularly helpful in orchestral playing because it helps me to project over the orchestra in solos and gives an intense point to my section in important tutti passages.

Some other practicing devices Mr.Robbins gave me follow.

Practice fast music with breaks

Practicing with breaks organizes fast moving material into what I call *units of release* which I will illustrate with passages from the first "Rococo" Variation and the Francoeur E major Sonata. (See Musical Examples 11 and 12) In the first Variation there are three entirely different bowing strokes in the first two measures. The first measure presents a string-crossing problem. The second measure involves a legato followed at the end by an up-bow staccato. Practicing with breaks enables one to relax and re-attack on each different motion. Returning to the original material, the feeling of relaxing in anticipation of a rest remains. This not only creates a definite musical plan that floats forward at very fast tempos, but creates the physical ease required to bring it off.

I applied a similar technique to Popper Etudes by elongating the last note of every three, four, six, eight, twelve, or sixteen (see Musical Examples 13 and 14, Popper Etudes no.4 and 12). In addition to creating *units of release* it established balance and security on the finger playing the last note of three, four, six, eight, twelve, and sixteen. I found this security a major gain in creating fluency and comfort in the execution of difficult thumb position passages in such works as the Schumann Concerto, the Haydn D major Concerto, the Dvorak Concerto, the Schubert "Arpeggione" Sonata, the Boccherini A major Sonata, and many other pieces.

Accent shifts

In the fast moving scales of the second "Rococo" variation (see Musical Example 15) and other similar passages, Mr. Robbins advised me to accent the shifts (usually first fingers) because it takes slightly more time to make a shift than to drop a finger. For some reason the bow arm seems not to know this and gets slightly ahead of the left hand. By accenting, however lightly, they are brought together at the critical moment.

Listen for the chord or tune produced by the first of three or four notes

Mr. Robbins pointed out that chromatic scales in sixteenth notes (four to a beat), as found in the fourth "Rococo" variation (see Musical Example 16), outline an augmented chord, while triplets (three notes to a beat), as found in the first movement of the Schubert B flat Trio (see Musical Example 17), outlines a diminished seventh chord. Listening for these chords makes the execution of these scales much more even and intonationally accurate. I found this particularly useful when, by extension, I applied the principle of hearing the chord or tune produced by the first of three or four notes to the passages in the Chopin *Introduction and Polonaise Brilliante.* In this piece I used "rhythmic" fingerings so that there was a shift on the first of two or the first of three notes. Then I practiced only the first finger notes and memorized by their sound and feel. This is what I concentrated on when executing the passage in its original version and found myself much more secure and accurate in performance. The memorizing of the first of four or the first of three notes and concentrating on the "tune" they create is effective in the execution of difficult, fast moving, orchestral material often found on audition lists.

Mr. Robbins introduced me to many concepts that dramatically and permanently changed the way I play and practice.

Feel the string through the bow

In an efficient bow arm one feels the string through the bow. In an inefficient bow arm, one feels the bow in the hand and moves it across the string without creating a connection between the body and the instrument. Mr. Robbins used three devices to create the ability to feel the string through the bow.

First, he had me move the bow against different textures (for example the rug on the floor and the wall) so that I could feel the difference. Next, he had me play sixteenth notes at the rate of quarter note = 138 (like in Popper Etude no. 6) (see Musical Example 18) so I would get a real sense of the "rub" of the bow on the string. After practicing this exercise for a week it doubled my sound in *detaché* passages.

Mr. Robbins also had me practice *collé* and up-bow staccato with various combinations of fingers on the bow.

Here are the three finger combinations:

1, 2, and 3 on, and 4 off
1, 3, and 4 on, and 2 off
1, 2, and 4 on, and 3 off
2, 3, and 4 on, and 1 off

These are the two finger combinations:

1 and 3 on (2 and 4 off)
2 and 4 on (1 and 3 off)
2 and 3 on (1 and 4 off)
1 and 4 on (2 and 3 off)

The exercises eventually create awareness of the fingers of the right hand as well as the left hand while playing.

Use bilateral transfer advantageously

Bilateral transfer is the tendency for one side of the body to influence the other. A negative example of bilateral transfer would be the tendency to let the bow come out of the string while making a difficult shift. Mr. Robbins would use bilateral transfer advantageously by concentrating on the work of the "easier hand;" concentrating on the bow and the relaxation of the right arm during shift, and concentrating on the vibrato oscillation during the length of a sustained note.

Pay attention when things are going well

It is important to pay attention when everything is working comfortably and correctly in order to develop a very clear picture of what comfortable and correct is. This attention creates an intellectual and kinesthetic database that can be accessed when trouble develops. This is of course distinctly different from being in a state of delight when one is playing well and going through painful analysis when things are going badly.

Practice one fifth lower to intensify tone

Practicing one fifth lower (on the next lower string) is particularly useful in the preparation of orchestral solos because it anticipates a greater bow pressure, which counteracts the tendency to play too lightly when slightly nervous.

Always warm up on slow pieces

Mr. Robbins often advised me to warm up on slow pieces such as *Arioso* by J.S. Bach, and *Vocalise,* by Rachmaninoff, and to use legato fingerings (see Musical Examples 20 and 21) in melodies as well as finger substitutions (see Musical Example 20) on the same note.

Practice in rhythms

Practicing in rhythms is probably the most effective way to get a passage into the fingers (see Musical Example 19).

Intonation

Translating fine intonation into English or any other language is an impossibility; however, three experiences I had helped me improve mine significantly.

Use a tape recorder

It is absolutely essential to use a tape recorder to check out what one might not be hearing. The tape recorder when properly used is a valuable tool. My experience is that the best results come when an entire performance is gone through and listened to later. In the case of auditions, I recommend playing the entire list every other day and listening to the tape on every following day. This strategy evolved during recital and trio tours. We would listen to the previous night's concert in the airport or car and make our mental notes. By the third or fourth concert, most of the easily-corrected flaws had been eliminated.

I do not recommend playing and listening to small segments over and over again. In the long run it tends to build in self-consciousness and an over anxiousness to please the microphone. This results in a loss of expression and sound. An absence of negatives is not a presence of positives.

Use the process of association to improve intonation

The second incident involved a very gifted student of mine whose artistry was constantly marred by slightly "off" intonation. Certain intervals were particularly bad, augmented 4ths and minor 6ths being the worst and most constant offenders. At one point, I asked him to play the first three notes of Maria from Bernstein's *West Side Story* (the first two notes of which form an augmented 4th). Amazingly he played it perfectly. I sent him home with instructions to find twelve tunes, one for each possible interval. From then on, every time he played out of tune, I would have him play the appropriate tune for that particular interval and then repeat the passage as written. The improvement was dramatic and within a few weeks, he no longer needed to refer to his interval list to maintain his newly acquired sense of pitch.

Relate the ear to the most stable notes

The third incident occurred at the Lyric Opera when we were doing *Lucia* with two different tenors. Placido Domingo decided to do the last scene one half tone lower throwing the cello solo from D major to D flat major. As I reworked the solo, I found it absolutely impossible to play it in tune until it dawned on me that in each key different intonational dynamics were at play. In D major, C sharp went to D, F sharp went to G and needed to be played slightly sharper to sound really in tune. However, in the transposition it sounded much better in tune when I thought of G flat relating to F and D flat relating to C and played these notes slightly flatter (see Example 23).

The reason this worked for me was that it was much easier to hear and feel F natural and C natural in the transposition and to relate the G flat and the D flat to those notes. In the original key, D natural and G natural were the stable notes, and it was easier to relate the C sharp and the F sharp to them. Enharmonic transposition works on the same principle.

Early on in my studies with Leonard Rose, he caught me playing out of tune. "There are several theories about intonation" he said, "Mine is very simple. I *listen* to myself. If I hear that I'm flat, I move the finger up but if I hear that I'm sharp, I move the finger down."

Mordant and simplistic as it seems, this advice stuck with me for a lifetime. For me, the main item was "I listen to myself."

Channing Robbins

Part V
Extra-Musical Aspects of Performing

In addition to the many stages of development one has to traverse in order to master an instrument well enough to become a performer, there are a number of psychological, professional, and spiritual elements that must be dealt with. To a large extent this chapter is written from my personal experiences and observations. In this regard every performer must create his own techniques and perspectives for dealing with nerves, career moves, politics, and self-sustenance.

The psychology of performing

Three good rules for successful performances: be prepared, give yourself permission to fail, and SHOW UP.

Be prepared

I earnestly hope that the information and techniques described in Chapters II, III, and IV will be of value to my readers. Being prepared to succeed in any venture is individual and in each case many factors are involved. Talent is an indefinable term but a definite reality when it comes to performing. Education, determination and persistence can turn a less than great talent into an excellent performer and the lack of any of these qualities will defeat even the most naturally gifted. Most important, however, is good judgment and good judgment is a result of experience.

My friend Scott Ballantyne often said that "common sense is common, but good sense is rare." Good sense mandates a step-by-step process to gain experience and confidence:

- Play from beginning to end without stopping alone (at home) and tape it.
- Play from beginning to end without stopping in front of one friendly person and tape it.
- Play from beginning to end without stopping in front of colleagues, conductors, or an audience.

At any point corrections and improvements can be made.

I was able to do multiple performances before my New York recitals and was often struck by the similarity between the *big* concert and all the little ones that preceded it. All the elements were essentially the same. Same repertoire, same order, same pianist, same me. All that conditioning was crucial to my believing that I could play well when it really mattered if conditions were in my favor and deal with any difficulties effectively if they were not. Mr. Rose spoke about playing entire recitals for imaginary audiences as part of his conditioning.

Early in my studies with him, I played my first important orchestral solo. The All City High School orchestra of New York scheduled *Le Roi d'Ys* overture of Lalo for its annual Carnegie Hall concert. I hardly gave its prominent solo a second thought. For that reason I was surprised when Mr. Rose demanded that I play it for him. After my rendition he played it for me amply displaying his usual virtues of gorgeous tone, perfect intonation, and elegant phrasing. After explaining and demonstrating on a note-by-note/phrase-by-phrase basis what he had done, why he had chosen to do it that way, and how he would practice it, he told me that he had played this very solo as principal cellist of the New York Philharmonic on the same program that Gregor Piatigorsky performed the Saint-Saëns Concerto, and intimated that, by preparing very carefully, he *did not* come out "second best." It became obvious to me that his playing was more a result of inspired "figuring out" as it was of the inspiration of the moment. He concluded the lesson by saying that "although you can never absolutely guarantee success in any given performance, you can put the odds in your favor" and added that he always came very early to every rehearsal in order to warm up and look over the material when he was a principal cellist.

Putting the odds in one's favor is very individual: Mr. Rose practiced long hours every day. Fritz Kreisler was famous for never practicing. Everything in this book up to this point is about being prepared. Prepared literally means PRE- before, and PAR- equal. Confidence ensues from the belief that we *are* equal to the task before we step out on the stage.

Give yourself permission to fail

Giving yourself permission to fail in no way means that one should try to fail, want to fail, like failing, or not prepare properly. It simply means acknowledging and accepting the fact that many things can go wrong no matter how well one prepares. This can be extremely empowering because fear of failure is the primary enemy of success. Failure itself can greatly aid success because it gives us valuable information.

For me, permission to fail is a psychological release from fear because having accepted failure, everything better is a plus and confidence increases. On the other hand NOT accepting failure means that anything worse than ones best expectations is a minus and sends confidence plummeting. In his groundbreaking book *Man's Search for Meaning,* Victor Frankl describes his experiences in a concentration camp. These real experiences are much worse than any imaginary experiences most of us can conjure up about performances no matter how important. The major conclusion he reached is that anyone can choose his attitude in any given situation. He called this "the last of the human freedoms."

We all have a choice about how we frame a situation in our minds. For the sake of our health (blood pressure, stomach ulcers, etc.) it is important to choose a point of view that allows us to do our best each time with the knowledge that only through experience can we improve it and eventually reach our potential (if not perfection). Perfection is by definition unreachable while excellence can be achieved step by step. It is also important to realize that we are not usually put into performing situations that we are unable to cope with. It is only reasonable to assume that our colleagues and employers know what they are doing when they engage us since our failure will damage their projects. Again good judgment is imperative to success and that is an individual call.

On one occasion, giving myself permission to fail turned a potential disaster into a fine success. I was warming up for a solo recital at Alice Tully Hall when I noticed a tremor in the middle third of my bow stroke. This was *not* a "shaky bow" due to nervousness but rather a fatigue symptom of over-practicing. A strange and bewildering feeling of fear mingled with extreme self-consciousness came over me. I started to speculate about the many very unpleasant consequences that would come to pass if I played badly.

My first reaction was to cancel the concert, but I gradually realized that the situation was not entirely hopeless. I knew that I was prepared and even if I did have to stop in the middle I would at least have the satisfaction and self-respect of knowing that I had done my best under impossible circumstances. When the concert began I was, in fact, very nervous, but no more than usual in such a situation and my confidence returned.

I was completely immersed in the music when I had a serious memory lapse in the fugue of the Bach C minor Suite. To my surprise, I wasn't in the least nervous. I simply couldn't remember how to get past my sticking point. This was not good, but compared to the horrors I had been envisioning before, it seemed minor. Before either going on to the Allemande or walking off stage to look at the music I looked out at the audience and said, "I'll try it one more time." The audience started to laugh and even I started to laugh. Fortunately I was able to get through the fugue and finish off the first half of the concert. All this time the tremor had continued to affect the middle third of my bow. And I felt enormously relieved that it had not in the least interfered with my execution of anything. The second half went without incident.

On many other occasions I faced performances on which my income and/or reputation were at stake. Needless to say, I prepared myself as well as was humanly possible for all these events, but I had to relinquish all responsibility for the outcome in order to "give my all" rather than "playing it safe." The two perspectives that helped me the most were:

1. I could live with the consequences of a bad performance, and
2. Nothing bad was likely to happen.

Show up

Although "showing up" seems axiomatic I can think of many cases where I almost didn't. One of these occurred when I was offered the American Ballet Theatre principal cello job. One day before the first rehearsal I was handed a pile of music containing seventeen ballets, some of which were very difficult. There was no doubt in my mind that this was more responsibility than I was capable of handling. Before calling the personnel manager and resigning instantly, my wife made an irresistible suggestion: "Let them fire you, but don't quit." As usual the actual situation was not nearly as daunting as I had imagined and I held the job for over thirty years.

Career development

The most important principle I ever heard on the subject of career development was articulated by the legendary conductor Leopold Stokowski in a speech at my wife's graduation from the Manhattan School of Music. In it he said that in Hollywood there are many actors who, although they are not great stars, are nevertheless always working. They are often character actors who excel in various stereotyped roles. He ended his talk saying "If you want to have a career in music, cast yourself well."

In music, like any other profession, the decision makers in every venue are not interested in alleviating anyone's unemployment problem but rather in satisfying some pressing need of their own. Two words spell the difference between success and failure:

Credibility and visibility

Potential employers must first know who you are and believe that you will be useful to them.

In his popular book *How to Win Friends and Influence People,* Dale Carnegie stressed the necessity of seeing a situation from the other persons point of view and relating to it in a way that satisfies his needs as well as your own.

In my years at the Lyric Opera I have heard many auditions both as principal cellist and two years as chairman of the audition committee. In that time I observed a great disparity in what pleased my colleagues and what pleased the music director. In order to please seven different musicians on the committee, personality and individual style seem to be a disadvantage. This was true to such a degree that I concluded that Jascha Heifetz would have been eliminated in the preliminaries (behind a screen) for demonstrating asymmetrical rhythm and an unblending sound. On the other hand our music director, Bruno Bartoletti, always favored players who were extremely expressive and very individualistic. This being the case, (and I believe it often is) one has to play quite differently in the preliminaries than in the finals in order to land a job. I would deserve to lose all credibility with my readers if I did not point out, that when between fifty to a hundred candidates show up for an audition and only one can win, the chances for any individual are remote.

In 1982 the American Ballet Theatre held auditions for a new concertmaster. The job of concertmaster is extremely important in a ballet orchestra. In addition to leading the first violin section in more than thirty-five ballets, the concertmaster regularly plays between 8 and 10 "stand up" solos (lasting five or so minutes). As part of the standard ballet repertoire the concertmaster must also play three major concertos (Chausson's *Poéme,* Mozart's *Symphonia Concertante,* and the Prokofiev Concerto No. 1) as well as the Bach D minor Partita.

Naturally there were many applicants for the position, but the resume of Dennis Cleveland, first violinist of the Audubon Quartet, really stood out. Even before his audition Mr.

Cleveland's credibility and visibility convinced us that we would be lucky to get him. Without this predisposition it is entirely possible that some other excellent violinist would have gotten the job. Dennis proved to be a wonderful Concertmaster and it was obvious that his years as first violinist of an important string quartet had prepared him well for the rigors of the American Ballet Theatre.

The best teacher I had in the area of career development was Paul Olefsky who was the principal cellist of the Philadelphia Orchestra from 1946-1950 and the principal cellist of the Detroit Symphony from 1954-1960. In addition to his orchestral career he won the Naumberg Competition in 1948 and the Michaels Award in 1952 (placing ahead of Van Cliburn). I first heard Paul Olefsky play during my last year at Juilliard. He played two concerts at Carnegie Recital Hall that were scheduled one week apart. Olefsky played both concerts brilliantly. His solo program included the Sixth Bach Suite and the Kodaly Unaccompanied Sonata, and his recital program included the Brahms F major Sonata and the Beethoven A major Sonata. His playing impressed me deeply, and I felt that that I could learn important lessons from him.

In the summer that followed these concerts, Paul Olefsky was engaged to teach cello at Kneisel Hall in Blue Hill, Maine. I was on excellent terms with Marianne Kneisel, Director of the school, so I managed to get a full scholarship.

Paul Olefsky was extremely encouraging to me and very generous with his time. He helped me to get my repertoire in order and continued to work with me after the summer for a fee so low that I could afford to study with him as much as I liked. The crucial advice that he gave me was to play in public as much as I possibly could. He advised me to learn pieces such as Strauss' *Don Quixote* and *Don Juan* by memory since they were likely to show up on audition lists. This was very helpful to me at my Lyric Opera audition where I did confront *Don Juan* as well as many other solos that I had memorized. He advised me to use every experience as a stepping-stone to being able to being able to handle greater and greater responsibilities.

When I was reluctant to audition for the principal cello position of the American Ballet Theatre in favor of practicing for competitions he told me in no uncertain terms that one principal position led to another, and that there were plenty of competition winners without jobs. When I failed to win a competition that offered a New York debut concert at Town Hall as its prize, he told me that many famous artists paid for their own New York debuts. He said that at this stage of my career I had both the money and credibility to do the same.

When my standing in the profession had risen sufficiently, Paul Olefsky helped me secure a job succeeding Channing Robbins as the principal cellist and chamber music instructor at the Dartmouth "Congregation of the Arts." This festival featured residencies by famous composers such as Kodaly, Ginastera, and Lutoslawski, and a first class faculty. From this experience I gained skill in the performance of contemporary music and had some fascinating interactions with great musicians. For me, Paul Olefsky's advice and direction in the early stages of my career created a synergy in which experience, preparedness, and credibility led to increasing opportunity. He also helped instill the mindset of taking my destiny into my own hands whenever possible. This attitude has served me well throughout my life.

Credibility can be gained either through endorsements from credible people, good reviews from credible newspapers or through associations with credible ensembles, orchestras, or companies. Credibility can be lost very quickly by playing badly. Every performer risks its loss at every performance. Long term survival in any venue where playing is constantly exposed is proof positive of adequate preparation

One final thought

I believe that the music of Schubert, Beethoven, Bach, Mozart, and others was divinely inspired, and that belief has sustained and enriched me throughout my life.

To spend one's life in the company of genius is the major compensation of being a musician.

Paul Olefsky

Part VI
Musical Examples

Cello Concerto

Ex. VI-1 Antonin Dvorak

Ex. VI-2

Sonata for Arpeggione and Piano in A Minor, D. 821

Franz Schubert

Ex. VI-3

Ein Heldenleben, Op. 40

Richard Strauss

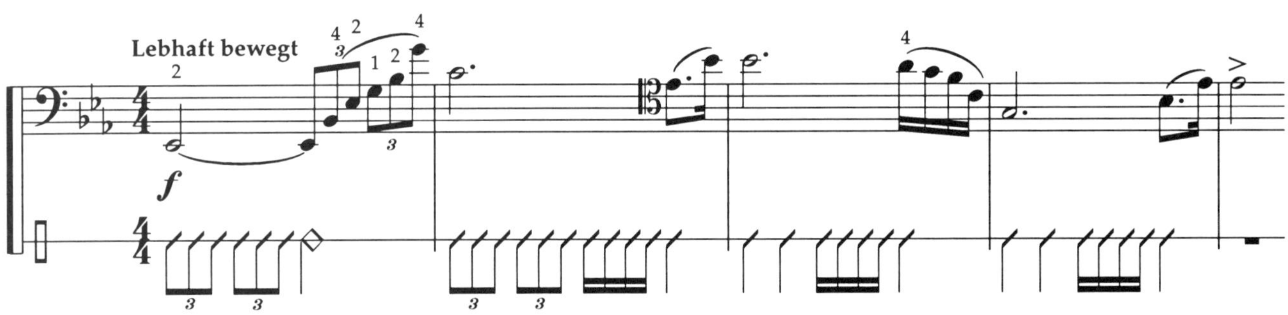

Ex. VI-4

Un Ballo in Maschera, Act III No. 7

Giuseppe Verdi

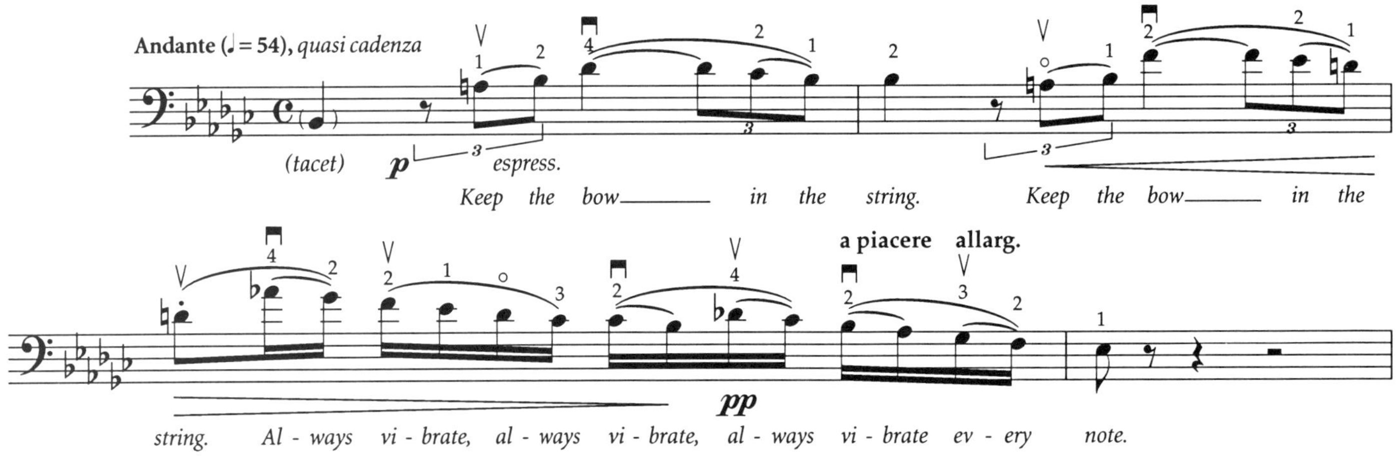

Suite No. 5 in C Minor, Fugue

J. S. Bach

Ex. VI-6

Suite No. 5 in C Minor, Gavotte I

J. S. Bach

Ex. VI-7

Suite No. 5 in C Minor, Gigue

J. S. Bach

Ex. VI-8

Ariadne auf Naxos

Richard Strausss

Ex. VI-9

La Sylphide

Ex. VI-10

Etude No. 26 (Forward and Backward)

Popper

original passage

first six notes repeated forward and backward

second six notes repeated forward and backward

third set of six notes repeated forward and backward

first two groups of six notes repeated forward and backward

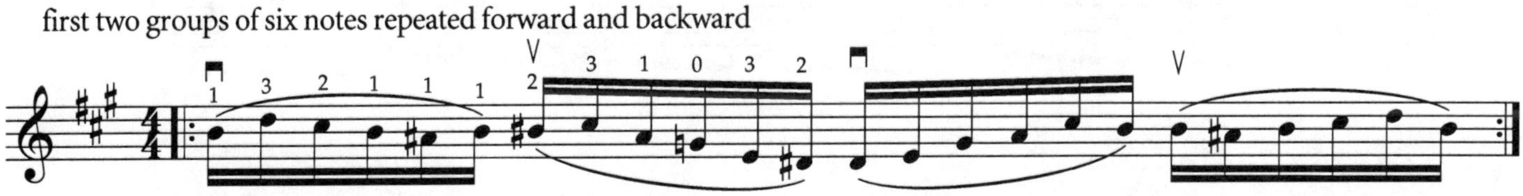

the whole measure repeated forward and backward

Ex. VI-11

Variations on a Rococo Theme, Variation I

Piotr Ilich Tchaikovsky

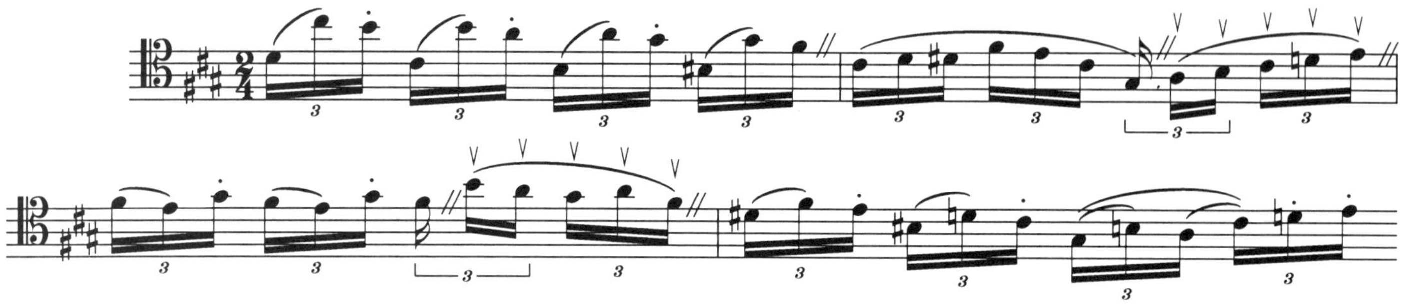

Ex. VI-12

Sonata in E Major

François Francoeur

Ex. VI-13

Etude No. 4

Popper

original passage

with added quarter notes

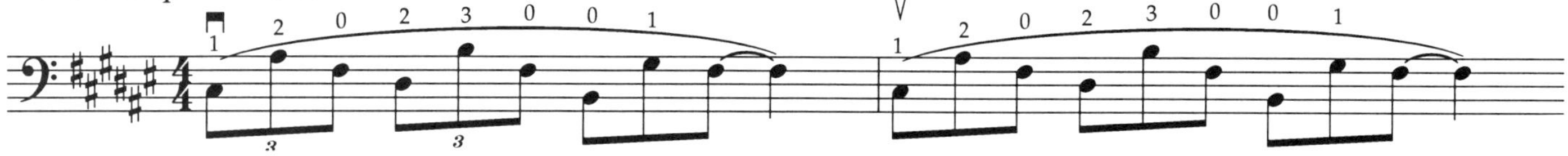

Ex. VI-14

Etude No. 12

Popper

original passage

with added half notes

Ex. VI-15

Variations on a Rococo Theme, Variation II

Piotr Ilich Tchaikovsky

for accenting shifts

Ex. VI-16

Variations on a Rococo Theme, Variation IV

Piotr Ilich Tchaikovsky

as it is in the piece

outlining the augmented chord

Ex. VI-17

Trio in B flat Major, Op. 99 D 898

Framz Schubert

original passage

chord outline

Ex. VI-18

Etude No. 6

Popper

original passage

with sixteenth note repetitions

Ex. VI-19

Etude No. 6

Popper

original passage

examples of rhythms

Ex. VI-20

Sonata No. 6 in A Major

Luigi Boccherini

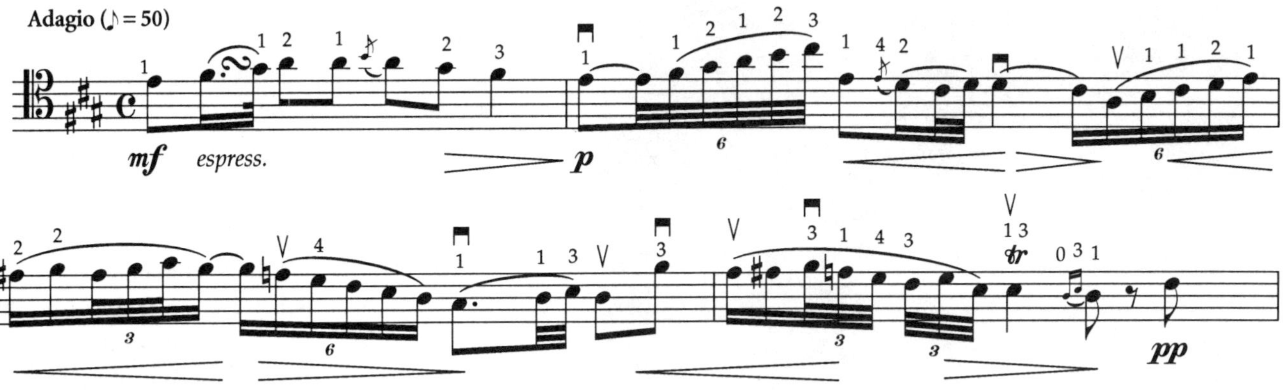

Ex. VI-21

Un Ballo in maschera, Act III No. 7

Giuseppe Verdi

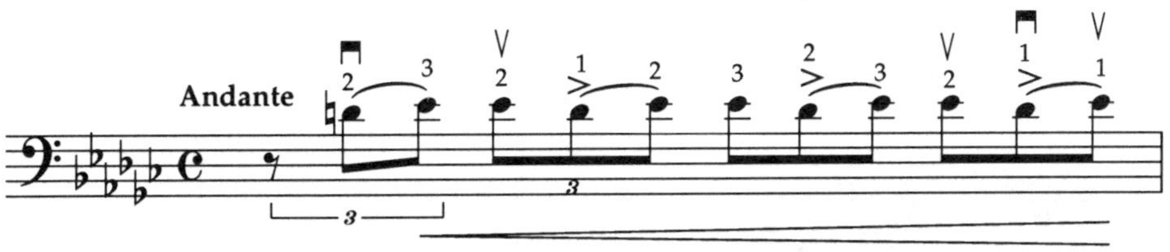

Ex. VI-22

Trio, Movement II

Piotr Ilich Tchaikovsky

Ex. VI-23

Lucia, Finale

Gaetano Donizetti

Daniel Morganstern has served as Principal Cellist for the Lyric Opera of Chicago and the American Ballet Theatre at the Metropolitan Opera House in New York for over thirty years. He has performed virtually every cello solo from the Opera and Ballet repertoire with such stars as Pavarotti, Domingo, Sutherland, Baryshnikov, and Markarova on national radio and television broadcasts.

Praised as a "first rate cellist" in the *New York Times,* he has presented most of the standard repertoire in his New York solo recitals which have included three at Alice Tully Hall, five at Carnegie Recital Hall, two recitals broadcast live from the Brooklyn Museum over WNYC, and others at the Lincoln Center Library, New York Cultural Center, and Cooper Union. As soloist with orchestra, he has played the concertos of Dvorak, Haydn, Boccherini, Tchaikovsky, Brahms, and Beethoven. Mr. Morganstern has toured extensively in solo recitals and as a member of the American Chamber Trio throughout the United States as well as in South America and the Far East.

He first received recognition at the age of 16 when he was awarded a scholarship by The Juilliard School of Music to study with Leonard Rose. In the same year, he was a winner in competitions held by the New York Philharmonic and radio station WQXR and made his debut with the Brooklyn Philharmonic playing the Boccherini Concerto.

Currently Artist Teacher of chamber music at Valparaiso University, he has been on the faculty of the Aspen Music School as well as the Dartmouth Congregation of the Arts and served as Principal Cellist of the Aspen Festival Orchestra, Joffrey Ballet and the American National Opera Company.

He has recorded with Eric Larsen the last three Beethoven Cello Sonatas, (Op. 69, and Op. 102, nos 1 and 2, HM 410), the Chopin "Introduction and Polonaise Brilliante," Schubert "Arpeggione" Sonata, and the Rachmaninoff Sonata (HM 727). With the American Chamber Trio, he has recorded the Complete Trios of Brahms and the "Archduke" of Beethoven (HM 630), Duos by Ravel and Kodaly, and the Tchaikovsky Trio (HM 619).

His edition of cello solos from the opera and ballet repertoire was released in 1999 by International Music Company for world-wide distribution.

So rewarding was Saturday's evening of cello and piano music—all of it by Beethoven—at Weill Recital Hall at Carnegie Hall, that one regretted missing its companion concert a week before. Rarely is this music allowed to speak in such a natural, buoyant voice.

New York Times

Morganstern's performance is primarily a virtuoso event. He opens with a fiery performance of a difficult arrangement of the Chopin Polonaise putting the cellist through feats of technical wizardry...

American Record Guide

For the mellow romanticism of Fauré's Elegy and Tchaikovsky's "Rococo" Variations, Mr. Morganstern was on firm ground, exploiting fully his warm, sweet tone, sophisticated sense of lyrical expansion and command of delicate color effects.

New York Times

These are very serious, technically polished readings of Beethoven's last three cello sonatas. This music demands much from its performers, and Morganstern and Larsen appear to give it their all.

American Record Guide

He opened with Francoeur's Sonata in E, a perfect choice since his gentle, warm tone gave each of the elegant movements a gracious lilt. There was much to admire also in the lyric sweetness he brought to Schubert's "Arpeggione."

The New York Times